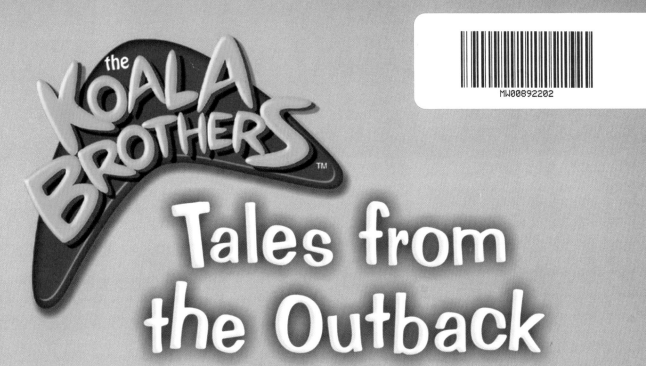

the KOALA BROTHERS™
Tales from the Outback

Adapted by Melissa Lagonegro
Based on the stories by David Johnson, Alison Brown and Diane Redmond

A GOLDEN BOOK · NEW YORK

Published in the United States by Golden Books, an imprint of Random House Children's Books, a division of Random House, Inc., New York, and simultaneously in Canada by Random House of Canada Limited, Toronto. Golden Books, A Golden Book, and the G colophon are registered trademarks of Random House, Inc.
Library of Congress Control Number: 2003022332
ISBN 0-375-82955-5 (trade)—ISBN 0-375-92955-X (lib. bdg.)
www.goldenbooks.com
Printed in the United States of America
10 9 8 7 6 5 4 3 2 1

Archie's New Home

One sunny day, in the middle of the outback, a little crocodile named Archie sat playing his ukulele. Archie had just moved to the outback. He was waiting for Frank to pick him up in his plane and fly him to his new home.

Archie was going to be the Koala Brothers' new neighbor, and he couldn't wait to get settled and make lots of new friends.

Meanwhile, Frank's brother, Buster, had his own job to do. He and Ned, the little wombat, had promised to clean Archie's new home by the water hole—but it was the scariest old house in the outback!

"D-do I have to come with you?" asked Ned.

"Well, I'm not going alone," replied Buster.

As Buster turned the handle to open the door, it made a creepy noise—**CREEEAAAKK!**

Frightened, Ned and Buster hurried back to the homestead. As Ned ran to hide in his trailer, Frank returned with Archie.

"Nice to meet *choo*, Mr. Buster!" said Archie as he shook Buster's hand.

The Koala Brothers then took their new neighbor to his house. Buster and Ned had not cleaned the house, but Archie didn't mind. He loved his new home! It wasn't scary to *him* at all.

Archie had an idea. He decided to invite everyone to a party at his house. So the little crocodile made some party invitations and mailed them out in town. Then he got right to work on the plans.

When the day of the party arrived, Archie was very disappointed. Only the Koala Brothers came—and he had hoped to make *more* friends.

"Look!" cried Buster. "Somebody's coming—it's Ned!"

Archie was thrilled, but as he opened the door to welcome Ned, it made a loud, creepy sound— **CREEEAAAKK!**

"No!" shouted Ned. "I don't like the sound of the scary door. Please don't open it!"

"That's the problem!" declared Buster. "Nobody came to the party because they're too scared to come to this creaky old house."

"I've got an idea," said Frank. "We'll help Archie fix up the house so it won't be scary."

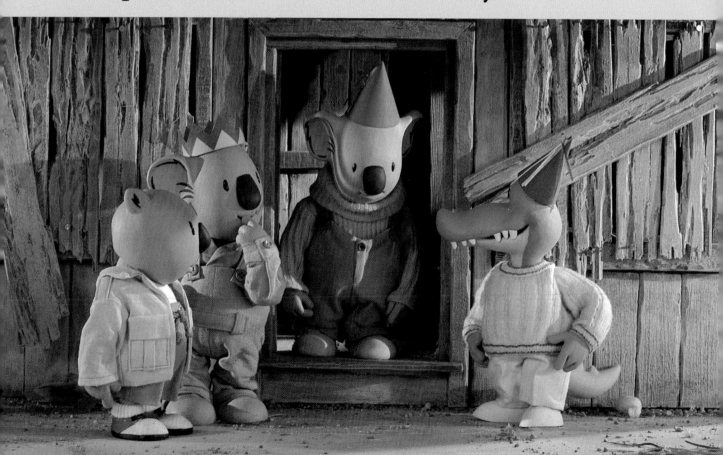

And that's just
what they did. Frank
painted the house . . .

Archie hung curtains in
the windows . . .

and Buster oiled
the squeaky old door.

Soon the house was finished. Archie was delighted.

"What do you think, Mr. Ned?" asked Archie.

"I . . . I like it!" replied Ned.

"Nobody could be scared of this place now!" said Buster.

With his house fixed up like new, Archie decided to have another party. This time everyone came— and no one was scared of Archie *or* his house again.

Thanks to Frank and Buster, the party was a big success, and Archie finally got to make lots of new friends.

The Thirsty Penguin

The outback is a very hot place—especially for a penguin. Penny, the little penguin, had been traveling and exploring all day under the hot Australian sun.

Penny was tired and very thirsty. But the little penguin soon discovered that her water can was empty. She really needed a nice cold drink—but it's not that easy to find one in the outback!

Meanwhile, Frank and Buster were out on their daily patrol looking for anyone in need of help. Suddenly, their plane made a spluttering noise.

"Uh-oh! Did you put fuel in the plane this morning, Buster?" asked Frank.

"No," replied Buster.

"Neither did I," said Frank.

So the Koala Brothers had to make an emergency landing.

"We'll have to walk home and get more fuel," said Frank.

But the Koala Brothers had a problem—they were lost!

As Frank and Buster were trying to think of a plan, the little penguin waddled toward them. They were surprised to see such a strange animal in the outback.

"Pleased to meet you," said Frank.

"Do you need help?" asked Buster.

Penny nodded and squeaked, pointing to her empty water can.

"Well, you're in luck," Frank told her. "We're here to help!"

"If only we weren't lost," said Buster with a sigh.

Luckily, Penny had a map. She helped Frank and Buster find their way back to the homestead.

"Now let's get you a nice cool drink," said Frank.

"And something to eat," added Buster.

But the Koala Brothers didn't know what she liked to eat—especially since they didn't know what kind of animal Penny actually was!

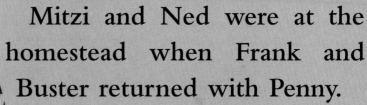

Mitzi and Ned were at the homestead when Frank and Buster returned with Penny.

"I think she's a duck," declared Mitzi. "Ned thinks she's a duck, too. Right, Ned?"

But Ned didn't answer. Frank and Buster looked in a book for the answer.

"Aha! I think I've found you!" exclaimed Frank. "You're a penguin!"

Penny squeaked and flapped her flippers in agreement.

"It says here that penguins like to eat fish," said Frank.

So Buster gave Penny some sardines, and the hungry penguin gobbled them down in a flash.

Now all Penny needed was a good rest. She unpacked her sleeping bag and fell fast asleep.

"She's so sweet," said Buster. "I hope she stays forever."

The next morning, Penny was ready to leave. But before setting off, she wanted to take some pictures of her new friends. And she had to help Frank and Buster find their way back to their plane. (Even the Koala Brothers need help sometimes.)

"Goodbye, little penguin," said Buster. "And thanks!"

Sometime later, George the postman delivered a letter to the homestead.

"It's from our little penguin friend," explained Frank. "Her name is Penny, and she's from Antarctica!"

"I hope she comes to visit us soon," said Buster.

"You know," said Mitzi, "I'm going to miss that duck."

Josie's Big Jump

One day in the outback, a little joey named Josie wanted to skip rope. Josie had never skipped rope before, but she was very excited about trying. She took a deep breath and a BIG jump.

"Arrgghh!" groaned Josie as she looked at the tangled rope around her feet.

Skipping isn't easy when you have big feet.

Just then, Josie heard a flip-flopping sound. It was her friend Mitzi.

"Hi, Josie," said Mitzi. "Will you skip to the water hole with me?"

"Uh, I can't," said Josie. "I'm busy. Maybe later."

"Okay, if I come back later will you promise to come skipping with me?" asked Mitzi. "Promise? Promise?"

"Yeah, okay, I . . . promise," replied Josie.

Josie let out a big sigh as Mitzi skipped away. Mitzi was a very good skipper. But Josie couldn't skip at all—and now she had made a promise.

Before long, Frank and Buster arrived at the general store to get some gas. Buster noticed that Josie looked sad.

"Are you all right, Josie?" asked Buster gently.

"I can't skip!" she cried. "And I promised Mitzi I'd go skipping with her later."

"Don't worry," said Buster. "We're going on patrol now, but we'll think of something. We're here to help!"

Josie tried skipping again, but she was still having trouble.

"Keep on practicing, Josie," said George. "Practice makes perfect!"

Josie took another big jump but got all tangled in the rope again.

"Just keep on practicing," said Alice. "Practice makes perfect!"

But no matter how hard Josie practiced, her feet kept getting caught in the rope. "Oh . . . I hope Frank and Buster can help me!"

Meanwhile, it was washing day at the homestead. Before going on patrol, Frank and Buster had asked Ned to hang their wash. When they returned, they found that poor Ned needed help, too! Ned didn't have enough clothesline to hang all the wash!

"We've got a problem," said Buster. But then he had an idea. "We need two ropes joined together to make one long line."

"Wow, Buster, you're brilliant!" exclaimed Ned.

Thanks to Buster's quick thinking, all the wash was quickly hung.

Suddenly, Frank remembered about Josie!

"Buster, we said we'd help Josie learn how to skip," said Frank.

"By this afternoon!" exclaimed Buster.

"Hmmmm . . . Buster, do we have any more rope?" asked Frank. "I've got an idea to help Josie."

Back at the store, Frank and Buster found Josie looking sad.

"How are you doing, Josie?" asked Frank.

"I've tried, but I still can't skip," said Josie.

"Well, we've got something that might help," declared Frank as he handed her two ropes knotted together. "If you've got big jumping feet, you need a long rope."

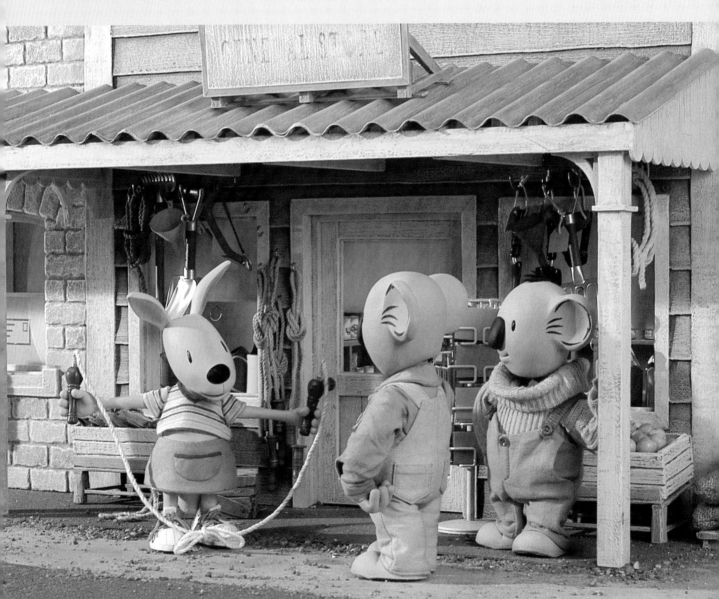

Josie didn't think the long rope would work, but she had to give it a try. She got into skipping position and . . . she skipped again and again and again!

"You've got it!" shouted Frank.

"You can do it!" cheered Buster.

"I CAN SKIP!" said Josie happily. "Thanks, Frank! Thanks, Buster!"

Before long, Mitzi returned to pick up Josie.

"Let's go skipping, Josie. Are you ready?" asked Mitzi.

"Yeah!" exclaimed Josie. "Catch me if you can!"

Mitzi was amazed. "I've never seen anybody skip as fast as you, Josie. You're the best!"

So, with a little help from the Koala Brothers, Josie learned to skip after all. And soon she became the fastest skipper in the outback!